A TELLING TIME

By Irene N. Watts

Illustrated by Kathryn E. Shoemaker

VANCOUVER • BOSTON

Rebeccah and Grandmother Esther watch the March wind blow flakes of snow across the moonlit garden.

"When I was a little girl in Vienna," says Grandmother Esther, "I remember an afternoon just like this one…

It was the day before the Purim festival, and I was on my way to the rabbi's house. Mother had been working hard to finish my costume in time.

I ran after the other children,
afraid I was going to be late,
afraid they would start without me.

But the rabbi himself opened the door in welcome. The stove in his study flickered warm shadows across the ceiling. We children sat close together, safe and happy to be inside, out of the snow and the streets that were dangerous places for Jews to be."

"That's why you came to live here, isn't it, Grandmama?"

"Yes. It was the last time we celebrated Purim in Austria, before the family left for the new country."

And so the rabbi began to tell the Purim story:

Long ago in the great land of Persia there lived a mighty king called Ahasuerus. Among his subjects was Mordecai, a judge and a loyal Jewish citizen. Mordecai had adopted his cousin Hadassah when she was orphaned as a baby. He loved her as if she were his own daughter and promised to watch over her always. To protect the little girl from those people who disliked the Jews, he changed her name to Esther, a name that was used by both Persians and Jews.

Messengers proclaimed the new law across the land.

Queen Esther sent her own servant to bring the dreadful news to Mordecai. When the servant returned to the palace, she told the queen that she had found Mordecai dressed in clothes of mourning, his face and hands streaked with ashes. She handed the queen a letter from Mordecai, which said:

I weep for our people, and beg you to go to the king and plead for their lives. Remember who you really are, Hadassah, and tell the king the truth.

King Ahasuerus had long been lonely without a queen to share his magnificent palaces, his gardens and his treasures. He sent for young women from all over Persia to be brought to the women's palace in Sousa so that he might choose a queen.

Mordecai took Esther to the palace, and they waited anxiously for the king to announce his decision.

The king chose Esther to be queen because she was kind and good and beautiful.

Mordecai, true to his promise, watched over Esther. One day he overheard some courtiers plotting against the king. He told Esther to warn her husband of the conspiracy. The king listened to his wife and banished the wicked men from the court. Then Mordecai's good deed was written down in the Royal Book of Records.

Haman was the name of the king's prime minister, and he was both powerful and cruel. People bowed their heads in fear when he walked by. But Mordecai refused to bow: "I bow only to the king," he said.

Haman's spies reported Mordecai's words to their master. Haman was so angry that he vowed to punish Mordecai the Jew and all his people with him.

He told his sons he would decide the day on which to kill Mordecai and his followers by playing a game of chance. The roll of the dice showed the number thirteen.

"This is the day the Jews shall die," Haman declared.

The rabbi's voice grew stronger. The sky had grown dark. The fire in the stove burned low.

Suddenly the door burst open. Soldiers entered.

"You are wanted for questioning, Jew," said the officer.

We huddled closer together, hardly daring to breathe. He looked at us.

The rabbi spoke. "Permit a little more time, sir, before you take me away; the children have not heard the end of the story."

I whispered, "Please let the rabbi finish."

The officer stared down at me, and then he looked up at the clock, at the hands moving slowly towards the hour.

"Fifteen minutes more, then your time is up," he told the rabbi.

And so the rabbi was allowed to continue, while the soldiers listened, the clock ticked, and the hands moved.

Haman went to see the king and warned him. "You are in danger from the Jews, who do not obey your laws but follow those of their own faith. I will reward anyone who helps us rid the land of Jews."

The king trusted Haman and gave him his own ring as a seal of his approval. Scribes were sent for, and Haman dictated these words:

When the moon is full, on the thirteenth day of Adur, let the killing begin. Death shall come to every man, woman and child of the Jewish faith.

Esther left the palace in disguise to visit Mordecai.

She brought him clean clothes so that he could enter the palace.

Mordecai refused them. "Will you speak to the king?" he asked Esther.

"I may not go to the king unless he sends for me. It means death to break the law," she said.

Mordecai replied, "Must we perish with all our people as Haman has commanded?"

Esther promised to try to find a way to help. She returned to the palace and wrote to Mordecai that she would pray and fast for three days. She asked him and the Jews to do the same.

I was chosen to be queen for one purpose, to help our people in their hour of need.

And so she made a plan. When the fast was over, Queen Esther dressed in her finest robes. She walked through the palace until she reached the great hall. Esther waited at the threshold until the king looked up and saw her.

"Queen Esther, what brings you here? You may speak."

"My lord, I have prepared a feast for you and Haman," Esther said, just as she had planned. The king and Haman agreed to go with the queen.

After they had feasted, the king asked Esther, "Tell me your wish. I will grant it, even if you ask for half my kingdom."

Esther replied, "Gracious lord, my wish is for you and Haman to feast with me again tomorrow."

On his way home that night, Haman saw Mordecai.

"Why do you refuse to bow to me?" he asked.

"I may bow only to God and to his majesty the king," Mordecai replied.

Haman was furious. He ordered his men to build a gallows.

Mordecai must die now. I shall
not wait until the thirteenth day
of Adur to kill him, he thought.

That night the king's rest was disturbed by the brightness of the moon and the sound of workers hammering the gallows.

The king opened the Royal Book of Records and read again the account of Mordecai's discovery of the plot against the throne.

This man should have been rewarded for his good deed. Why was it not done?

The next day he summoned Haman and asked him how he would reward a subject's loyalty. Haman thought the king intended to honour him. Eagerly he replied, "I would clothe this man in the king's own robes and let him ride the king's horse through the city."

"An excellent plan. Arrange the procession for Mordecai," the king said.

The following day Mordecai rode while Haman walked, forced to listen to the people cheering his enemy.

That night, Esther held the second feast. The king asked her to tell him what was in her heart, and this time Esther felt free to speak.

"I am doomed to die with all my people, for I also am a Jew."

"Who dares to say my queen and her people must die?" the king thundered.

Queen Esther pointed to Haman.

Haman fell to his knees, grasping the hem of the queen's robe. "Oh pity me," he cried.

The king called his guards, "Remove the tyrant who threatens my queen and her people. He has deceived me and must die."

Haman was taken to the gallows that he had built for Mordecai. And Mordecai was made the new prime minister.

As the thirteenth day of Adur approached, Esther reminded the king of the danger to the Jews. The king told her that even he could not break the law once it had been proclaimed. "But," he said, "I will permit the Jews to defend themselves against attack."

The Jews were saved, and so we remember this day with gratitude. We celebrate the courage of Queen Esther on the festival of Purim, by dressing in costume, waving noisemakers and stamping our feet. We eat pastry in the shape of Haman's ears, called hamantaschen. You see, children, the story has a happy ending.

The rabbi smiled at us. The officer looked from the clock to the rabbi. "You have five minutes left. Send the children on their way," he said, and turned his back.

Our rabbi led us out into the lamp-lit street. Snowflakes fell. He gave us his blessing, waved goodbye.

When I reached the corner, the rabbi had vanished."

"What happened to him?" Rebeccah asks her grandmother.

"Who can tell? A miracle occurred that night, just like the miracle of Purim. And somewhere, I believe, the rabbi still tells the story of Queen Esther."

For Rebeccah and Meghan—INW

For Judi, a gifted teacher—KES

Published simultaneously in 2004 in the US and Canada by TRADEWIND BOOKS LIMITED **www.tradewindbooks.com**

Distribution and representation in the UK by TURNAROUND www.turnaround-uk.com

Text copyright © 2004 by Irene N. Watts • Illustrations copyright © 2004 by Kathryn E. Shoemaker

Book Production by ELISA GUTIÉRREZ

Prepress by *Disc*, Vancouver, British Columbia

LIBRARY AND ARCHIVES CANADA CATALOGUING IN PUBLICATION

Watts, Irene N., 1931-
    A telling time / by Irene N. Watts ; illustrated by Kathryn Shoemaker.

ISBN 1-896580-39-4 (bound).--ISBN 1-896580-72-6 (pbk.)

    I. Shoemaker, Kathryn E. II. Title.

PS8595.A873T44 2004   C813'.6   C2004-903387-5

Printed and bound in Korea   10 9 8 7 6 5 4 3 2 1

The publisher thanks the Canada Council for the Arts and the British Columbia Arts Council for their support.

Canada Council   Conseil des Arts
for the Arts   du Canada

BRITISH
COLUMBIA
ARTS COUNCIL
Supported by the Province of British Columbia

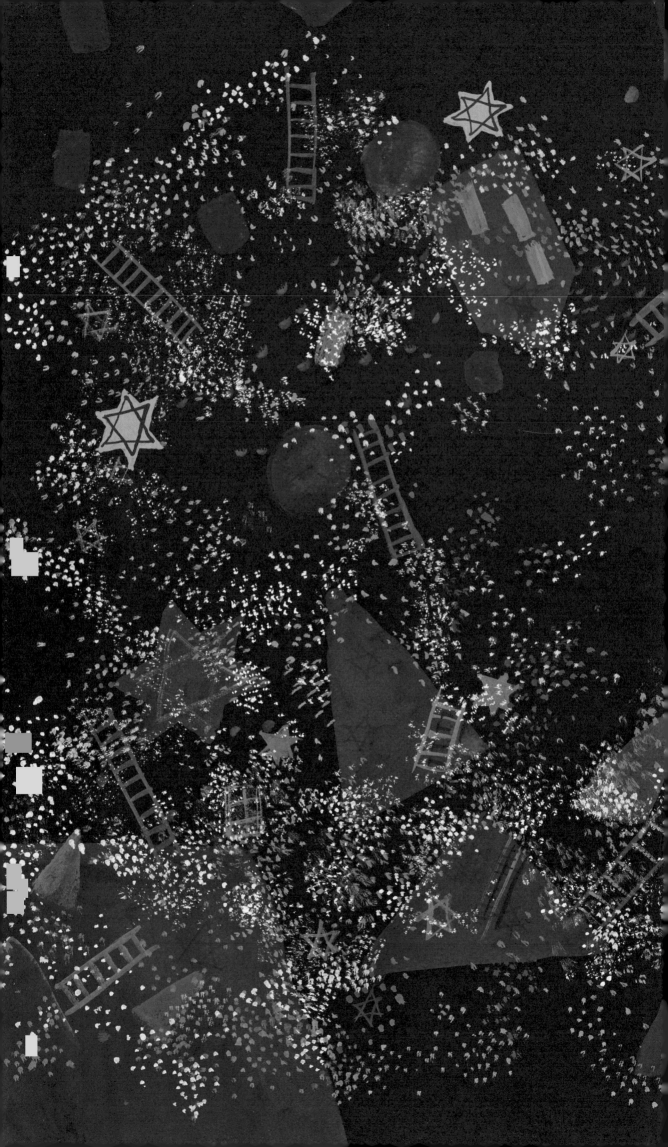